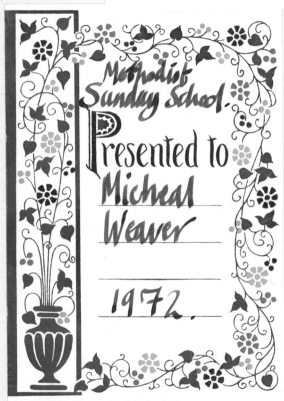

Methodist Sunday School.

Presented to

Micheal Weaver

1972.

THE BOOK ROOM, 7 Carrs Lane, Birmingham, B4 7TG

STORIES IN THIS BOOK

A LADYBIRD 'EASY-READING' BOOK

Stories about
Jesus the Helper

by HILDA I. ROSTRON

with illustrations by CLIVE UPTTON

Publishers: Wills & Hepworth Ltd., Loughborough

First published 1960   ©   *Printed in England*

HELPING THE
BLIND MAN

Long ago there lived a blind man. He lived where trees and flowers grew; but the blind man could not see the trees or flowers.

The poor man had to feel the way to go with his stick. Tap-tap-tap went his stick on the road. He walked slowly.

7214 0057 4

Each day the blind man sat by the side of the road. People who were sorry for him gave him money to buy food.

The blind man heard the footsteps of people passing by.

There were different sounds of footsteps. He knew when children ran and skipped and danced along.

One day the blind man sat listening.

"I hear many footsteps passing by. There must be a big crowd of people to-day. Where can they be going?" said the blind man to himself.

Then he called aloud, "Where are you going?"

"Jesus is coming! Jesus is coming!" they told the blind man.

The blind man had heard of Jesus. He knew that Jesus made people well and happy. He knew that Jesus loved children.

"If only Jesus would help me. He will if I ask Him," thought the blind man.

He took hold of his walking stick and stood up.

"Jesus, please help me! Jesus, please help me!" called the blind man. But Jesus did not hear. The blind man shouted even louder.

"Jesus, please help me! Jesus, please help me!"

"Do not make such a noise," said the people. But the man shouted still louder.

And Jesus heard him.

"Bring him here to Me," said Jesus. So they led the blind man to Jesus.

"Why did you call? What do you want Me to do?" asked Jesus.

"Please, Lord Jesus, make me able to see."

Jesus put out His hand and touched the man's eyes.

He opened his eyes and saw the kind face of Jesus.

HELPING THE DEAF
AND DUMB MAN

Everybody loved Jesus because He made them well and happy. The people who had been helped talked about Jesus to their friends.

There was one man who could not hear and could not speak. This made his friends sad.

They wanted to tell him about Jesus and how He helped people.

One day friends of the deaf and dumb man came to see him. He watched them talking to each other.

"I wonder what they are saying," he thought. He wished he could hear.

Then they took his hand and led him outside the house. Together they walked down the road.

Along the road they saw a crowd of people. The deaf and dumb man wondered what the people wanted.

Jesus, the One Who helped people, stood there.

The poor man was led by his friends to Jesus. He turned His head and smiled at the deaf and dumb man.

Then the friends of the deaf and dumb man spoke to Jesus. They were asking for something.

"What a kind smile He has," thought the poor man. He watched them all and tried hard to understand.

He *wished* he could hear what they said. He *wished* he could speak.

Jesus took the deaf and dumb man's hand and led him from the crowd. The poor man wondered where they were going.

When they came to a quiet place, Jesus stood still. The deaf and dumb man stood still, too.

Then Jesus gently touched the man's ears and tongue.

Jesus looked up at the sky.

Soon the man heard sounds. He heard the sound of the crowd.

He heard Jesus speak; and the man found he could speak as well.

Perhaps the happy man said, "Thank You for my ears to hear and for my tongue to speak."

HELPING THE
CRIPPLED WOMAN

There was a woman who was a cripple. She could not see the sky because her back was bent. She saw the flowers and the grass. She could not see the tall trees.

She saw the birds hop on the ground. She could not see them fly up high.

People were very sorry for the poor woman. They helped her along the road. She had to walk slowly with two sticks.

Perhaps the children helped. They could run and jump and climb. They could pick flowers and run messages for her to make her glad.

One day Jesus went to church. It was up a hill. Many people went to the church and were following Jesus up the hill.

Strong people walked fast. They liked to climb the hill. The children ran up the hill to see their Friend Jesus.

Old people walked slowly up the hill.

The poor woman with the bent back took a long time to climb up the hill. She had to stop and rest many times.

She walked very slowly, step by step. At last she was at the church door.

She went into the church and stood there behind the people.

The people stood up and sang praises to God.

Then Jesus stood and read out of God's Book. Everyone listened to Jesus.

Jesus looked at the faces of the people in front of Him; but He could not see the face of the poor woman with the bent back.

Jesus was sorry. He wanted to help her to stand up and walk like other people.

Jesus asked her to come near. He gently touched her bent back and told her to stand up.

She found she was able to stand up. Jesus had made her well. She was glad and sang a song of praise.

HELPING THE
LITTLE GIRL

Jesus helped many people. He loved to help the children as well as grown-up people.

Jesus had friends who were fishermen. They lived near the Sea of Galilee, and had fishing boats.

One morning the sun shone in the blue sky. The boats sailed on the blue sea.

Jesus was with His fisher-men friends in one of the boats. The boat sailed near to the shore.

The people on the shore saw Jesus.

"Look," they called to each other, "Jesus is coming! Jesus is coming!"

The children ran and called to each other, "Jesus is coming! Jesus is coming!"

Soon the boat came to the shore. A big crowd of people were waiting.

Children were paddling near the edge of the water. They saw Jesus smiling at them.

Jesus loved the children and the children loved Him.

Everyone wanted to be near Jesus to hear what He would say.

One man tried hard to get closer to Jesus. The man's name was Jairus.

He looked very sad because his little girl was ill.

"Make way for Jairus," the people said to each other. "He wants to ask Jesus for His help."

So at last Jairus came close to Jesus.

Jairus said to Jesus, "My little girl is very ill. Will You please come and put Your hands on her and she will be well again."

Jesus went at once.

Someone came running to tell Jairus, "Do not bother Jesus to come. Your little girl is dead."

Jairus looked at Jesus.

"Do not be afraid," said Jesus. "Trust Me."

Jesus went with Jairus into the house. Jesus stood by the little girl's bed, took her hand and said, "Little girl, get up."

She sat up, smiled at Jesus and her father and mother.

Jesus said, "Give her something to eat," and smiled.

Series 606A